Alex and Lulu

Mix and Match

To Ivan, for always sharing colours with me – L.S.

A TEMPLAR BOOK

First published in the UK in 2009
by Templar Publishing,
an imprint of The Templar Company Limited,
The Granary, North Street,
Dorking, Surrey, RH4 IDN, UK
www.templarco.co.uk

First edition

ISBN 978-1-84877-000-3

Thanks to Milo Leeb-Domina, Luca and Roman Brogno
and Annie Tsou for their wonderful drawings.
Designed by Mike Jolley
Edited by Libby Hamilton

Printed in China

Alex and Lulu

Mix and Match

by Lorena Siminovich

templar publishing

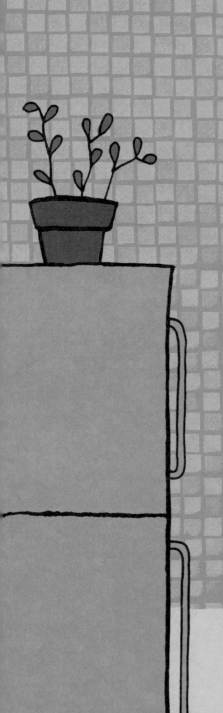

Today, Alex and Lulu's kitchen table is covered
in paint, paper and glue.
"What's going on Lulu?" asks Alex.
"I'm trying to make a **collage**," sighs Lulu,
"but it's not going right."

"Yesterday, Mrs Lawrence told our
class about the school art competition,"
says Lulu. "The theme is
My Biggest Inspiration,
so our picture is supposed to be
about the special things that make us
want to paint or draw or collage."

"I want to make a collage of the peacock we saw at the wildlife park," says Lulu. "But I just don't have the right colours!"

"I need the colours in my imagination – juicy **green** for the grass, magnificent **blue** for the body and shimmery **pink**, bright **turquoise** and all kinds of **purples** for the feathers."

Lulu looks at her collage. The colours are **sludgy**,
not bright... not right. A big tear rolls down her cheek.
"It's nothing like the picture in my head."

But Alex has a great idea.
"Come on Lulu," he says. "Let's go for a bike ride."

Alex and Lulu cycle all over town – through the park, past the café and, just by chance, they end up outside the bookshop.

Alex has a secret plan. As soon as Lulu is busy with her bird book, he creeps upstairs to a special department...

Art Supplies! It sells all kind of special paper
and paints. Behind the counter is Miss Flora.
"Hello Alex," says Miss Flora. "What can I do for you today?"

Alex looks around at all the **different** colours.
"I need some green, turquoise, blue, shimmery pink and all kinds
of purples, please – Lulu is doing a very important collage."

Miss Flora and Alex look at all the different kinds of paper and paint.
Alex chooses so many that soon his arms are tired from holding them!
But something important is worrying him.

"Miss Flora," he says shyly, "there might be a bit of a problem..."

Over at the counter, Alex takes out his pocket money.
They look at the pile of paper and paint, and then at
the little pile of coins in his hand. It isn't enough.

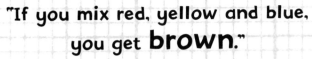

"If you mix red, yellow and blue, you get brown."

Yellow

Red

Blue

"And if you add white, the colour gets lighter – mix red and white to get pink!"

White

Red

What a great idea.
Alex buys four pots of paint
and lots of different kinds of paper.

The next day, while Lulu is at her friend Sara's house,
Alex starts to paint the paper. Sometimes he paints himself
by mistake, but soon Alex is surrounded
by papers of **every** colour.

Yellow

"Oh Alex, what have you done?" says Lulu,
coming back and seeing multi-coloured Alex.

Alex shows Lulu all the different coloured papers he has made for her.

"This is **perfect!**" says Lulu. "Now I can make my collage
just like the picture in my head and win
the school competition!"

Lulu starts work on her new collage straight away.
Alex trys to keep his eyes open, but it has been a long day.
Before long he falls asleep at the kitchen table.

A little bird flys down to the window and gets Lulu thinking – maybe she has a **bigger** inspiration than the peacock, right in front of her?

Red

The next day, Lulu has finished her collage and Alex wants to see it.
"No Alex, don't look — I want it to be a surprise," says Lulu.

Lulu walks to school with the collage rolled up tight.
Now and then Alex tries to sneak a peek.

At lunchtime, Alex can't wait to hear how the competition has gone.

In the playground he runs up to Lulu.

"Lulu! Lulu! Did you win?"
Lulu looks a bit sad.
"No Alex, I didn't win," she says.
"But today it's my turn to
give you a suprise..."

The walls of the school hall are covered in all sorts
of pictures, with bright colours everywhere.
There is a big painting with a large, red, first place
rosette stuck on. But Lulu drags Alex past it.

Thomas

Mati

Lulu

Charle

In one corner is a little painting,
covered in bright bits of paper.
Alex gives Lulu the biggest hug.
"Who cares if you didn't win, Lulu —
your painting is the **best** ever.
And I'm your biggest fan!"

Lulu

To Alex, my biggest inspiration.
Lulu

The end